The
Three Li'ili'i Kittens

by Elita H. Keener

Gloriamaris Publishing

First edition 2022
ISBN 978-0-578-28880-2 (hardback)   ISBN 978-1-0880-3293-0 (ebook)
Published by Gloriamaris Publishing

for my keiki, Lionel and Wesley

The three li'ili'i kittens, they messed their mumus...

And they began to cry, "Oh Mother dear, see here, see here! Our mumus we have messed!"

"What! Messed your mumus, you
naughty kittens! Then you shall
have no poi."
"Meow, meow, meow."
"No, you shall have no poi."

The three li'ili'i kittens, they washed their mumus and hung them out to dry. "Oh mother dear, see here! See here! Our mumus we have washed."

"What?! Washed your mumus? You good little kittens.
Then you shall have some poi. Meow, meow, meow! Yes, you shall have some poi."

The three little kikes, they lost their snorkel masks, and they began to cry,
"Oh, mother dear, see here, see here! Our masks we have lost!"

"What! lost your masks? You naughty little cats, then you shall have no beach."
"Meow, meow meow!"
" No, you shall have no kahakai.."

Those three little kittens, they found their masks and they began to cry, "Oh mother dear, See here! See here! Our masks we have found."

"What?! Found your masks, you good little kittens, then we shall go to the beach!

"Meow, meow, meow! Yes, we shall go to the kahakai!"

The three little kittens, they lost their Hawaiian slings
and they began to uē. "Oh, mother dear, see here! See
here!
Our Hawaiian slings we have lost!"
"What!? Lost your slings? You naughty little things,
then you shall have no poke."
"Meow, meow, meow!"
"No, you shall have no poke."

Those three li'ili'i kittens they found their slings and brought their mother fish. "Oh, makuahine dear! See here, see here! Our Hawaiian slings we have found." "What!? Found your slings! You good little things! Then you shall have some poke."
"Meow! Meow! Meow!"
"Yes, you shall have some poke."

The three liʻiliʻi kitties, they lost their ukuleles and they began to cry, "Oh mother alohaʻia, see here, see here! Our Ukuleles we have nalowale."

"What? Lost your ukuleles? You kolohe kitties, Then you shall have no luau."
"Meow. Meow. Meow."
"No, you shall have no luau."

The three little kitties, they found their ukuleles
and tuned them GCEA. "What, found you ukuleles!? You maika'i loa little kikes.
Then you shall go to the luau." "Meow, meow, meow!" "Yes, you shall go to the luau."

The three little kittens, they lost their leis
and they began to say, "Oh, mother dear,
see here, see here, our leis we have
misplaced!"

"What?! Lost your leis, you naughty kittens! Then you shall have no pork. Meow, meow, meow. No you shall have no pork."

The three li'ili'i kittens,
they relaced their leis,
and they began to cry,
"Oh mother dear, see
here, see here, our leis
we have remade."
"What? Remade your
leis? you good little
keikis, then you shall
have some pork!"
"Meow, meow, meow!"
and they got out their
forks.

Those three li'ili'i kitties they strummed their ukies
and they began to sing,

"Oh mother dear, see here, see here,
your li'ili'i kikes love you so!"

Then she began to purr,
"Aloha, what a day my aloha'ia little kittens.
But I think bedtime's near!

Meow, meow, meow.

Yes, I think bedtime is near."

KAHAKAI

BEACH

uē (ooway) cry

Aloha

hello

Li'ili'i
Little

KIKE
KITTEN

CONTEXT

When you come to a word you don't know, you guess it based on the rest of the sentence and story.
That is called context!

U
K
U
L
E
L
E

Poi

- Taro root, peeled and steamed
- water

Mash Taro root and add water til smooth and sticky. So Ono! (Yummy)

Aloha means a brotherhood of love and peace

MAKUAHINE

MOTHER

MUMU

Hawaiian dress

MAHALO
THANK YOU

lei
flower
necklace

maika'i loa very good

aloha'ia beloved

Hawaiian sling
rubber band powered harpoon for hunting fish

'Ohana family

nalowale
✕ lost ✕

How many hawaiian words did you guess correctly?

THE HAWAIIAN ISLANDS

KEIKI CHILDREN

kihi-kihi

Ka'a Car

POKE poe kee

marinaded raw tuna

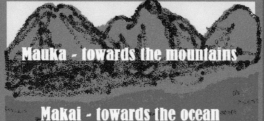
Mauka - towards the mountains

Makai - towards the ocean

PŌPOKI CAT

humuhumunukunukuapua'a

reef triggerfish

Luau- hawaiian party

aloha!

goodbye!

kolohe  mischievous

Printed in the USA
CPSIA information can be obtained
at www.ICGtesting.com
LVHW071304041123
763053LV00006B/7